Billu Leaves India!

Billu Leaves India!

Memories of a Boy's Journey

Gersh Subhra

Illustrated by Iain MacLeod-Brudenell

Matador
9 Priory Business Park
Kibworth Beauchamp
Leicestershire LE8 0RX, UK
Tel: (+44) 116 279 2299
Fax: (+44) 116 279 2277
Email: books@troubador.co.uk
Web: www.troubador.co.uk/matador

ISBN 978-1783062-027

British Library Cataloguing in Publication Data.
A catalogue record for this book is available from the British Library.

Typeset in Palatino by Troubador Publishing Ltd

Matador is an imprint of Troubador Publishing Ltd

This book is dedicated to my *Tyaa*, Lachman Das Subhra who I left behind in India in 1964. The happy stories about the time I spent with him as a child inspired this book.

To my parents who made the incredibly brave decision to travel to England with four children and £2 pounds in their pockets!

Acknowledgements

This book has been a collaborative effort with many people providing encouragement and support. Two friends in particular, have been incredibly generous in donating their time:

Iain MacLeod-Brudenell

Iain is a long-standing friend and former colleague at the University of Derby who has worked in education with just about every age group from nursery to university students. Iain, like Billu, loved drawing as a boy.

He is now a multi-media artist using video, printmaking, sculpture and drawing in his work.

You can see his work on www.iainmacleod-brudenell.com

Ken Holland

Ken's support has been invaluable in getting this book to print.

He has worked in social care, health and education for many years and recently set up his own company, VOX (UK) CIC, supporting individuals and organisations to achieve better quality of life outcomes. Ken has creative skills in IT, multi-media and digital music and along with his work with VOX, provides digital media support to groups and organisations.

You can see the work of VOX at www.voxcommunityinterest.org.uk

All profits from the sale of the book will be donated to:

The Derby Open Centre

Established in 1981, the Open Centre is a well respected organisation based in Derby in the East Midlands. We exist to promote understanding between different communities by celebrating and raising awareness of their faith and cultural heritage. We promote good community relations between British citizens, no matter what their background or beliefs. As part of our activities we work closely with many different communities, faith organisations and places of worship as well as representatives of secular organisations; however the Open Centre is not a religiously based organisation and has no affiliation to any specific faith based groups.

www.derbyopencentre.org

Oxfam

"Oxfam is a global movement of people working towards a world without poverty and we won't rest until we get the job done. We respond fast in emergencies and stay to help people re-build their lives. We work on long-term projects with communities determined to shape a better future for themselves. We campaign for genuine lasting change. It starts with one simple fact: all human lives are of equal value and full of potential. Experience tells us with the right support and training, people can work their own way out of poverty."

www.oxfam.org.uk

"Oxfam are grateful and delighted to be one of the beneficiaries of this book. I hope you enjoy reading Billu's exciting and touching story as much as I know Gersh has in writing it."

Ron Lodge, Senior Fund-raising manager, Oxfam

Introduction

During the 1950's and 1960's many families from India, Pakistan and the Caribbean made the momentous decision to come to England and start a new life. This was at the invitation of the British government that was facing a serious shortage of workers in many industries. The decision to emigrate was often very sudden and meant leaving loved ones behind for a long time. Fathers often travelled by themselves with just a few pounds and spent a number of years working in order to save up the money for the cost of air tickets for the rest of the family.

'Billu Leaves India' tries to capture a child's perspective to emigration and the complex mixture of emotions involved in leaving a familiar place. His family in India has a web of relationships that stretches between grand-parents, uncles, aunts and cousins. The close relationship that Billu has with his cousin and uncle act as the focal point of this story and the gift of a seemingly magical copper bowl from his beloved uncle offers a chance to keep these memories alive when he is in England.

Chapter One

Billu loved living in India!

He lived in Banga, a small village in the north of India.

He was only six years old but he knew every corner of his village. Billu would go out exploring every day, his mum called it 'going on his *sehra*'. Billu's *sehra* always involved looking for new things to draw. He was often seen around the village with his notebook and a bag of sharp coloured pencils, sitting on a wall, outside the school or in his father's sweet shop.

Billu's older brother, Narinder, often asked Billu why he always smiled whilst drawing.

Billu would just reply, "I'm happy, aren't you?"

Billu had a favourite cousin, Pummy, who lived next door to him. Pummy was Billu's favourite because they had been born on the same day! Billu was born in the afternoon and Pummy in the evening. Narinder would often tell Billu about that day.

"I was so excited that a baby was being born and when they said

there were two boys, I ran and shouted it all around the village! By the time I got back home there were about twenty children running after me! *Daddyji* gave out sweets to everyone that day."

Every morning before Billu set off on his *sehra* he would pack a small picnic, containing a stuffed cauliflower chapatti (a *gobi paraata*) and an orange sweet called a *jalebi*. His mother would always call out to him as he left.

"Don't go too far! Stay with your cousin Pummy! Make sure you stay in sight of the house!"

Billu would hear all of this and know that there was nothing to worry about. His father's six brothers and their families all lived in the same village, and they would wave to him wherever he went.

Billu had two brothers, Nita and Narinder, and a sister called Suman, but he would never go out on his *sehra* with them. The only person who could go with him was Pummy, who Billu often thought of as a brother as well.

Every day Billu would draw pictures of the multi-coloured peacocks that landed gracefully on top of the tall houses in the village. Billu would call out and stare at them intently, trying to get them to look in his direction.

It seemed to him that the peacocks knew they were being drawn by the way they strutted and spread their grand tail feathers. They caw-cawed loudly, as if to say to Billu: "Concentrate and draw us properly!"

When he had finished, Billu would hold up the notebook for them to see. He was pleased when they nodded their heads and flew off gracefully into the sky.

Another thing that Billu liked to draw was his favourite uncle, who he called his *tyaa*. On his *sehra*, Billu would always call in on his uncle for a glass of his favourite milk drink, which is called a *lussi*. His *tyaa* would have it ready for him and would watch Billu drink whilst he looked at his nephew's latest drawings.

Tyaa would spend every day crouched in front of a wooden table with a small hammer, making copper bowls from shiny, flat, metal sheets. The rhythm and ring of the hammer was quite hypnotic and Billu would often sit and watch him for hours at a time. The bowls had small dimples in them and Billu thought they were magical because they reflected your face a hundred times. He often wondered if his *tyaa* was a magician, because he could make the bowls so quickly and they were always perfectly round.

Chapter Two

One day, after having spent all day out with Pummy, Billu came home to find his mum sitting on the edge of her bed, crying. Narinder sat next to her and he was also crying, his head bowed and tears falling silently onto his bare legs.

Billu was surprised to see his father standing in the corner of the room. His father usually came home from the shop much later than this and Billu immediately knew that something was dreadfully wrong. Tears started to well up in his eyes, even though he didn't yet know what was wrong.

Narinder looked up through red eyes and said, "We are leaving India!"

Billu's mum and dad looked at each other nervously. His mum's crying grew louder and Billu rushed to her, bursting into tears as well.

"What do you mean? Where are we going? What has happened?" Billu's head was full of questions, because he didn't really understand what 'leaving' meant.

His father moved to a chair, called Billu to him and sat him on his knee.

"We have a chance to go to England. My friends are going and they have asked me if we want to go with them."

Billu could see tears in his father's eyes. He had never seen his father cry before and he began to feel scared. "Is it a bad place? Can I still draw there? Can I take Pummy? Can I come back to see *Tyaa* in the afternoon?"

The questions came flooding out of Billu, and each one seemed to make his mother cry louder.

"I don't want to go," she said. "We have four children and we are happy here! Why do we have to leave?"

Billu's father looked down at the ground, but before he could say anything a voice behind him spoke. "Think carefully about making the decision to go. You will be leaving everyone behind."

Billu turned to see that *Naniji*, his grandmother, had come into the room. She was a tiny woman with a quiet voice, but today it seemed much louder and almost angry. He ran to her and clutched at her *shalwar* trousers.

"I'm scared *Naniji!* I don't want to go, I love India! Tell them we don't have to go. Will you be coming?"

Naniji picked the small boy up and held him tightly as he sobbed. Billu had known the answer to his question before he had even asked it.

"No *puttar*, my special little child. I won't be coming with you, but you know that I will wait for the day that you come back."

Billu realised that leaving for England meant not seeing the people he loved for a long time. It gave him an aching, empty feeling in his stomach. Suddenly the room felt very cold and Billu squirmed out of his *naniji's* arms and ran out of the room without looking back. He saw his notebook and pencils lying on the ground outside and grabbed them as he sprinted away from the house. As he ran, images of the things that he loved about his village filled his mind. He desperately wanted to draw them, just in case he never saw them again.

Chapter Three

A short time after he had ran away, Billu found himself at his *tyaa's* house. It had a big door with ornate patterns in beautiful shades of red and brown. It had a big, round handle, which was the same copper colour as the bowls that his *tyaa* made. He had tried to draw this door many times but, despite concentrating hard, he had never managed to get the patterns quite right.

Billu began to kick and bang on the door, calling out to his *tyaa*. His efforts pushed open the door and he ran upstairs to where his uncle was calling. He found him sitting on a large bed, or *manja*, in front of the only window in the room. Usually *Tyaa* would scoop his small nephew up into his arms whenever he came to visit, but today he remained seated and staring out of the window. Billu sensed immediately that his *tyaa* had already heard the news of their leaving.

"Tell *Daddyji* not to go, *Tyaa*! Who will look after me if you don't come with us?"

Tyaa turned, his eyes filled with tears. "*Namaste*, hello, Billu. Come and sit down with me." *Tyaa's* long arm rested on Billu's shoulder and he spoke softly. "Your father wants to help you all get a wonderful

education. There are good schools and universities in England. He has been given a chance to work there and to make a better future for all of you."

As he listened, Billu began to think again about all of the different things that he wanted to capture in his notebook before he left. His small fingers clutched the notebook and he closed his eyes tightly to make the images of India clearer in his mind.

Tyaa realised what Billu was thinking and gently asked, "Tell me Billu, what will you miss the most about India?

As the small boy began to talk quietly, his *tyaa* picked up a shiny metal bowl from the window ledge. It was the shiniest one that Billu had ever seen, it was almost as if the sun's rays that came through the dusty glass had polished the dimples on the surface. He placed the bowl gently on Billu's lap and held the boys hands in his.

"There will be no-one to draw the peacocks!" Billu began. "You know how they love being shown their pictures. They will be cross if I don't go to see them every day." As Billu spoke, soft petals of tears fell and landed in the bowl. He heard them make a soft, deep sound, which sounded far away. "I won't be able to play in the cornfields or swim near the well."

Billu recalled how the farmers would pump water from the wells into the fields, or *keth*. The children of the village would run and splash in the water, and their laughter would ring louder in the air as more and more joined in. Their brown skin would turn a deep red from the colour of the rich, fertile, Punjabi soil, and the farmers would smile whilst pretending to be annoyed by the children's antics. The aroma of wet soil would cling to the air, along with the spray of the water.

Afterwards, the children would lie on the roof of a small white farm building and dry their bodies in the hot Indian sun. Often they would listen to the men discussing the prices of crops and land. Billu suddenly remembered how the conversations would often turn to the families that had left for England. He recalled that they had talked about families not returning for a long time.

"What about the barber?" suggested *Tyaa.*

Billu smiled as he thought about the barber, the *nayee* who had a little shop opposite his *tyaa's* house. He loved to go into the shop with Pummy and ask the *nayee* to cut their hair. When he wasn't busy, the barber would sit both of them in big, red, leather chairs that had foot pedals, which pumped the boys high up into the air! Then he would pull out white sheets and tie them around their shoulders like capes, pretending to cut their hair with shiny scissors that went clickety-clack.

Billu thought that the scissors sounded like small birds as they flew through the air above their heads.

The best part was always the red, yellow and orange striped sweets that the *nayee* gave to them afterwards. Billu and Pummy would pretend to pull imaginary coins out of their pockets and flick them to the *nayee* as payment. He in turn would pretend to catch them. Memories of the *nayee* caused more tears to flow as Billu realised that Pummy would be staying behind in the village.

"What is this, *Tyaa*?" Billu asked, as he looked down at the bowl on his lap.

"This bowl is special and it's for you, Billu." *Tyaa* spoke quietly as he wrapped it in a crisp, white cotton cloth. "All of your memories of India will stay in it. As you grow older memories of England will fill your mind, but the bowl will help you to remember what you love about India. Look deep into the bowl and your memories will come back." *Tyaa's* rough, long-fingered hands gently held Billu's small, soft, brown hands. "Hold the bowl when you feel sad in England. Look at the dimples on the surface and you will see all of our faces. Hold the bowl against your face and you will feel India's sun. When you need courage, hold it to your chest. Remember, you are not leaving India, a part of it is coming with you."

Billu looked at his *tyaa's* sad face, which was full of long, deep lines. They seemed much deeper today and Billu wondered how long he would remember his kind face.

Chapter Four

Billu and his *tyaa* sat quietly on the *manja* bed and stared at the shiny copper bowl. The dimples reflected small images of the boy and the old man so clearly that Billu wondered if his *tyaa* had actually drawn them onto the bowl!

"Can we go to the marketplace and get our favourite *kulfi* ice-cream, *Tyaa*?" Billu asked excitedly. It seemed to him that going about their daily routine was the only way Billu would lose the heavy sadness that he felt in his stomach. "Can I sit on your shoulders? Can I pick a mango from the tree? Can I wave to *Daddyji* as we pass his shop? Is there a newspaper that we need to buy today?"

All of the things Billu loved to do came flooding out as he was hoisted up onto his *tyaa's* shoulders. His *tyaa* was one of the tallest men in the village and so when Billu was on his shoulders he felt like he was sitting on top of the world!

They strode down the busy Railway Road and waved to all of the shopkeepers, who were sat outside talking to their customers. They eventually passed the sweet shop where Billu's father worked and Billu jumped up and down on his *tyaa's* shoulders excitedly. His father looked

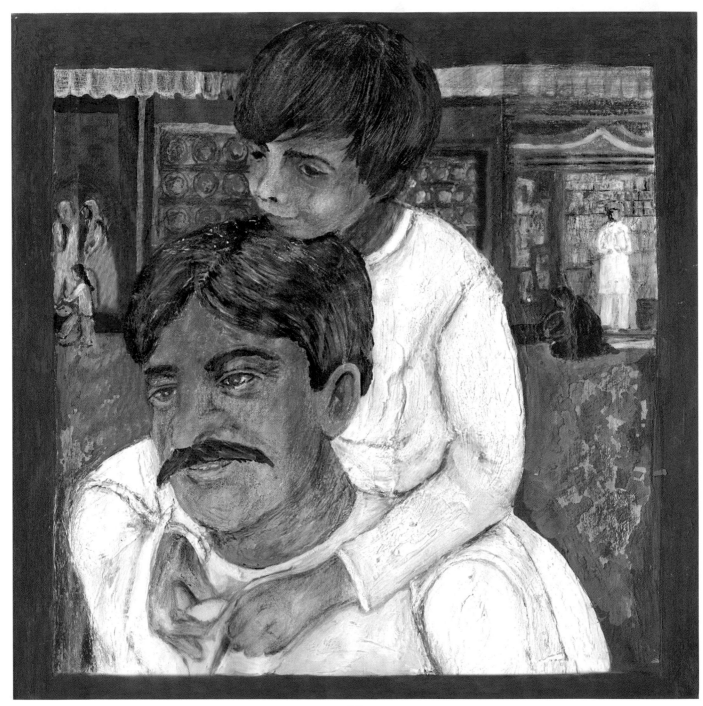

16

up and smiled broadly at him. His black moustache made him easily recognisable from the crowd of men that were in the shop.

"So Billu, which flavour *kulfi* ice-cream is it to be today?" asked *Tyaa*.

"Pistachio! Pistachio! Every time!" Billu shouted.

"Pistachio it is. But what shall I have?" *Tyaa* knew the answer before it came.

"Mango! Mango!"

Billu loved the game of choosing ice cream. The choice of flavours never changed and the shopkeeper always had the two ice-creams ready and waiting as the tall *tyaa* strode up with the boy on his shoulders.

As they walked through the busy market, or *mundi*, Billu noticed that his *tyaa* was walking much more slowly than usual. His long legs usually carried them through the *mundi* at a brisk pace, but today his *tyaa* was pausing at each shop and describing the things that were on sale to Billu.

"Look Billu! Look at the sweets that the man has made today. The sweets, the *matayee,* are so colourful! Look Billu! Look at the big sacks of rice. Shall we have rice for dinner today?"

Billu looked this way and that, trying to take in all of the images that surrounded him. The colours, the smells, the noise all seemed to be so much more vivid today. He held up his bowl and wished that it would capture all that he could see.

Chapter Five

The following morning Billu awoke to the sound of the village peacocks caw-cawing. He was filled with excitement as he planned where he would go with Pummy, what he would draw and which flavour *kulfi* ice-cream he would have that day. He changed out of his pyjamas quickly and was about to run next door to Pummy when he saw his sister, Suman, sitting outside. She was playing with the ribbons of her dress and looking down at her sandals, or *chappals*.

Billu walked over to her and saw that her face looked sad. Her sadness encouraged Billu to invite her on his *sehra*, something he had never done before.

Suman shook her head in reply to his invitation. This puzzled Billu, as she usually always wanted to go along with the two boys. Then the memory of the yesterday's discussions about leaving India crashed back into Billu's mind and his sister's sad face suddenly made sense.

"I don't know what England will be like," said Suman. "But we will all be together and that means it will be OK."

"No it won't!" shouted Billu angrily. "Pummy, *Tyaa* and the peacocks are staying behind. It's not fair!" Billu ran back into the house and jumped onto his bed, the *manja*, and wrapped himself in the cotton sheet, the *chuddar*. He heard his sister follow him into the room and sit down on the edge of the *manja*.

"What's this Billu?"

Billu pulled back the *chuddar* from his face and saw Suman holding the copper bowl that his *tyaa* had wrapped in the white cotton cloth. He sat up and rested the bowl on his knees. "It is how I will remember India," he said.

Suman looked puzzled. As he unwrapped it, Billu remembered how he had held *Tyaa's* rough hands when they had spoken about the things that he loved most in India. "*Tyaa* said that I should put my memories of India in here, so that I don't forget the peacocks and my *sehra*," he continued. "What will you want to remember, Suman?" Billu asked excitedly.

His sister looked a little less sad now, as she became curious about the shiny copper bowl. "I want to remember the flowers here in the village," she said. "You know how much I love their colours and smells."

Billu thought fondly of how his sister would come home from school each day with an armful of colourful flowers. White jasmine and orange marigold flowers were her favourites, and she would sit on the floor for hours making garlands, or *haar*.

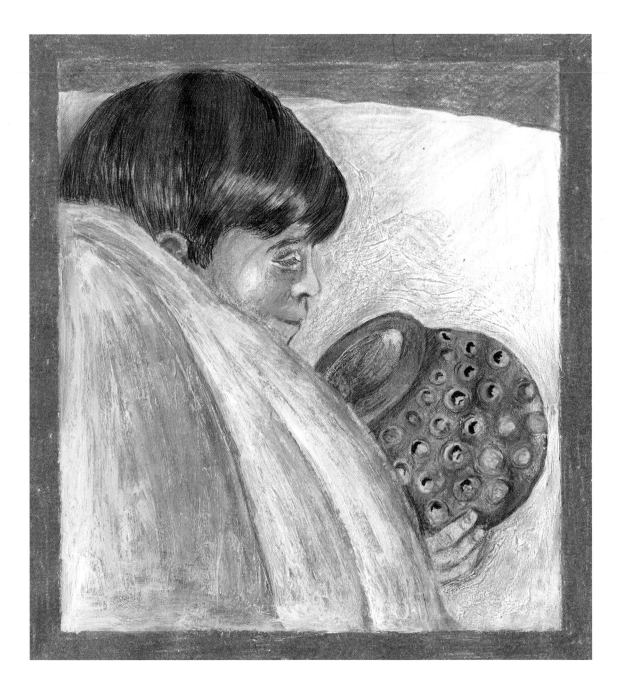

21

"Let us put some flower petals into the bowl!" exclaimed Billu. "The bowl will remember their smell and you can remember the flowers when we are in England!"

As Suman ran off to collect some flowers, Billu sat quietly and tried to remember what else he loved about India. As he looked around he saw the narrow alleyway, or *gullee*, next to his house. It was dark and the air was always very cold and still. Very few children went through this *gullee* as the darkness scared them. However, Billu and his *tyaa* often walked through it, as it led to his house. Billu picked up his bowl and walked to the *gullee* entrance. He stood in the darkness of its doorway and called out to his *tyaa*.

"*Tyaa, Tyaa*, are you there?" Billu waited before calling again. "*Tyaa*, are you working outside? Can you come and fetch me?

Soon a reply came back down the dark *gullee*. "Come Billu, come and run as fast as you can!"

Billu had never gone down the *gullee* by himself before, but today he felt brave and he wanted to show his *tyaa* that he could do it. He started running, his left hand trailing on the damp stone wall. He usually closed his eyes when he walked through with his *tyaa,* but today he kept them wide open. The bowl, which he clasped tightly against his chest, seemed to give him a new sense of courage. The damp air suddenly began to

warm as Billu neared the end of the *gullee*. Sunlight flooded through and when he reached the other end his *tyaa* scooped him up with his long arms and placed him gently on his shoulders.

"I did it! I made it! I didn't close my eyes! I was really brave, *Tyaa*!" Billu shouted.

Tyaa held Billu's feet tightly as the little boy jumped up and down on his shoulders.

"Well done! Well done! *Shabash! Shabash!* My brave *puttar*, my brave little boy! I knew you could do it. Did the magic bowl make you brave? Did it make you run faster?"

Billu held the bowl high in the air and let the bright Indian sun send sharp reflections dancing across his face.

"Yes it did, and when I am in England I will hold it always. Thank you for making it for me *Tyaa*."

Billu's *tyaa* smiled broadly when he heard this. His own sadness was lessened by the little boy's excitement and newfound bravery.

Chapter Six

The day they would leave India was now not far away. Billu's house saw many visitors come and go: some were friends wishing the family well; some brought gifts and others sought advice about how they too could begin to make plans to leave India for England. None, however, had discouraged the family to leave. All seemed to be joining in the excitement that had begun to fill Billu's home.

Narinder regularly brought back stories of England from his school in the village and he would sit and share them with a group of little children around him. He would spread his arms wide and dramatically recount the stories that others had told him.

"Did you know there is cold, white powder that falls from the sky and turns to water when it touches the ground?" said Narinder, excitedly.

Billu's eyes widened when he heard this, not really knowing whether to be impressed or scared.

"Did you know that it is so cold there that you have to light a fire inside the house?" Narinder could see that he was making Billu more and more curious with his stories, so he continued telling what he had heard at school from children with relatives living in England. "Did you know that there are black rocks that burn brightly on the fire in the room that you sit in? You have to store these black rocks in a room under your house!" Narinder tried to sound as if he understood what he was saying, but he didn't really know that cellars were rooms used to store coal under houses in England.

"Is there any sunshine to keep us warm, or any peacocks in England?" asked Billu nervously.

"Don't be silly, of course not! It's far too cold for the sun and the peacocks have long flown away to warmer places like India or Africa."

Narinder was really enjoying Billu's nervous questions, but inside he was also getting an uneasy feeling that perhaps England was going to be a very different place to India.

Billu wondered why his parents hadn't chosen this place called Africa. A country with peacocks seemed much better than one with cold, wet powder falling from the sky.

In the days leading up to the departure, Billu kept himself busy by sketching pictures of all the things he loved most about India. In addition to the many pictures of peacocks, his *tyaa* and the barber's shop, there were now also images of his house, the farmer's fields and his grandmother, *Naniji*.

28

Tyaa had shown Billu how to draw as soon as he could hold a pencil and provided him with a regular supply of notebooks. He could see that Billu had a real talent for capturing the images around him and encouraged him to draw every day. As Billu filled these books with his colourful drawings, *Tyaa* had put them in a wooden box for safe-keeping. He intended to pass them onto Billu's father to take with them to England.

Into this box he added a letter of his own. Some of what he wrote in the long letter described the joy that Billu had brought to his life. *Tyaa* had never married and so had no children of his own. He had many nephews and nieces, but Billu had always been his favourite and they had spent so much time together.

He wrote:

My dearest Billu,

Have wonderful dreams about your future, make them exciting and full. Do not be sad in your heart when you remember where you have come from, let the memories be happy ones. See the past as your foundation and your source of strength; build on this foundation and your future is sure to be filled with happiness and love.

Tell your children about your old Tyaa and tell them about your magic bowl. Look deep into the bowl to remember your memories of our time together.

I will always remember you.

All my love,

Tyaa

Chapter Seven

Finally, the day to leave India arrived. Everyone had woken early, just as the peacocks had begun to call to each other. Billu's younger brother Nita had been the first one awake and, although he was only three years old, he sensed the excitement of the day. He ran from room to room, singing, asking questions and jumping onto the suitcases. Billu, Suman and Narinder were all much quieter, trying to be helpful but often getting in their mother's way as she tried to gather last minute things for the long journey.

Pummy had stayed at Billu's house for their last night in India. He, like Billu, was quiet and stayed by Billu's side throughout the morning. He looked down at his feet and pushed his hands deep into his pockets, feeling around for the peacock feather that he had picked up the previous day. He took it out slowly and tugged at Billu's shirt.

"Take this to England, Billu," he said kindly. "Use it to help you draw lots more pictures of peacocks."

Billu looked at Pummy and saw how sad he was. He wished that Pummy was coming along with him. He couldn't remember a single day when they hadn't been out together on their travels or on a *sehra* around the village. He was glad that his *tyaa* and Pummy were coming to the airport.

Finally everyone was ready to go and it seemed that the entire village had heard of their leaving. People stood in their doorways to wave and Billu waved back at the many familiar faces.

The railway station was busy and it took some time to find seats for everyone. Billu sat next to *Tyaa* on the train and held his hand tightly. He clutched his notebook on his lap and looked at some of the images that he had tried to draw in the station. One of the station inspectors who knew his father had taken Billu to the front of the train so that he could meet the driver. Billu saw a man putting black rocks into a fire and realised that this is what Narinder had been describing about keeping warm in England. Billu had quickly tried to draw the fire as the driver wished him good luck for the journey to England.

The journey to Delhi Airport was going to take about ten hours and there they would meet more family relatives, who were coming to see them off. *Tyaa* began to talk about one of his brothers who had joined the Indian Navy and had travelled around the world on big ships. He was going to be at the airport and Billu remembered how this uncle always

told wonderful stories about the different places he had visited whenever he came back to the village.

Narinder, who up until now had been unusually quiet, began to talk about England. "Billu," he said excitedly. "Did you know that you will be starting school when we get to England?"

This filled Billu's head with a flood of questions. Who would take him? Who would be in his class? Would he sit next to Narinder? Would the teacher be from India? How would he learn to speak English?

Narinder, as ever, began to enjoy Billu's worried expression. "I can speak some English," he boasted and began repeating words that he had learned at school. His teacher had encouraged him to do this after hearing of his family's decision to leave India.

Narinder began reciting some words and pestered Billu to repeat them. This effort was too much for Billu; the words sounded so different from the Punjabi language that he spoke. In frustration, he turned and buried his face into his *tyaa's* white *kurta* shirt.

"I don't want to go, *Tyaa*," he whispered quietly. He didn't want Narinder to hear him. His older brother didn't seem at all sad about leaving.

Tyaa wrapped his long arms around Billu and whispered to him. "Be brave, my *puttar*, my child. Hold the bowl tightly and it will make you look forward to being in England."

Billu had forgotten about his shiny bowl in the excitement of the day but now he pulled it out of his bag and ran his fingers across the many dimples on the shiny surface. *Tyaa* was right, it made him feel braver. He looked across the rail carriage and saw that Suman had brought a small bag of flowers and was making a garland. She stepped down from her seat and placed some of the pink petals into the bowl and hugged Billu. Billu was glad that he had an older sister like Suman. He decided that in England he would like to begin going on *sehra* with her.

Chapter Eight

Finally the family arrived in Delhi, the capital city of India. The railway station was big and noisy, with people pushing in all directions. Everyone seemed to be carrying bags, suitcases or parcels and were either starting or finishing a journey. Billu tried to identify who might be going to England like them.

A shout from someone in the crowd jolted Billu from his thoughts and he was relieved to see the familiar face of his uncle, who worked for the Indian Navy. His smart blue uniform made him stand out in the crowd. He picked Billu up and let him wear his navy cap.

The whole family travelled in a large taxi to the airport and, as they went through the centre of Delhi, their uncle told the children about his latest travels, which had included going to England. He told them about the fast, modern trains, the beautiful countryside and the palace where the Queen of England lived. He said that he had stood outside her house and tried to count the number of windows but had to stop at one hundred! Billu's eyes became wider and wider at the thought of such a house. "Do they have peacocks there, Uncle?" he asked.

His uncle looked puzzled by the question and began to talk more about his recent trip to England. "I know that you love going on *sehra* around your village, but England has lots of fields and parks where you can play with your friends." He looked at the bowl that Billu was clutching tightly. "Your t*yaa* has told me about this bowl and how you think it is magical by the way it makes you feel brave. Do you think it can make you feel excited about going to England? Why don't you hold it tight, close your eyes and imagine what the countryside will be like?"

Billu closed his eyes and held the bowl close to his face. As before, it seemed to become warm and suddenly he could see clear images of green fields and animals eating grass. This particular animal seemed to be covered in white fur! Billu opened his eyes wide and wondered where the image had come from.

"What did you see, Billu?" his uncle asked.

"I saw the countryside! I saw green fields! I saw white animals! It was beautiful! But I don't know what the animals were?"

Billu's uncle smiled and explained that the animals were sheep, which were covered in white wool. He too began to wonder if *Tyaa's* bowl really was magical, because of the way it seemed to make Billu see such clear images. His thoughts were interrupted by a shout from Narinder.

"There's the airport!"

All the children swung round to see the white building and beyond it the enormous aeroplanes. The whole family fell silent as they realised that their journey really was about to begin. Billu looked across at his father, who had been quiet throughout the journey from their village. He turned and smiled at the little boy, stroking his hair softly.

"Be brave my *puttar*, my son," he said.

"I am *Daddyji*, I have *Tyaa's* bowl with me and it is making me brave." Billu tried to sound as confident as possible, but his stomach seemed full of butterflies. The idea of getting onto one of those big, metal aeroplanes and leaving India was now becoming very real and very scary.

The airport seemed to be even busier than the train station, and the next two hours of waiting to check into their flight with people pushing past carrying enormous suitcases became all too much for Billu. His tears began to flow when he and his family had to move into another room, leaving *Tyaa*, Pummy and his uncle behind.

"I don't want to go! I want to stay with you, *Tyaa*! Let me stay, I don't want to leave India!" He pulled his hand from his mother's tight grip and ran back to his *tyaa*. The airport staff ran to bring him back, but Billu had wrapped his arms tightly around *Tyaa's* neck.

Billu's navy uncle spoke quietly to the airport staff and asked if he could escort the family to the aeroplane with *Tyaa*. This wasn't usually allowed, but the staff could see how upset Billu was and the official navy uniform of his uncle persuaded them to make an exception.

Slowly, the family made their way across to the big, white Air India plane. Narinder was running at the front, pulling Nita alongside him. Suman was holding her mother and fathers' hands and Billu was high up on his *tyaa's* shoulders, but holding his navy uncle's hand as well.

As they got close to the plane, Billu's father took him from *Tyaa's* shoulders and carried him up the steps to the door. Billu looked back and realised that his *tyaa* was not behind them but had stepped back from the plane and was waving. The little boy reached into his bag and held the shiny copper bowl high in the air.

"I love you, *Tyaa*! I'll be brave. I will always remember you, *Tyaa*!" he shouted.

40

Glossary

BILLU   A popular Punjabi boys' name

BANGA   large town near the city of Jullunder, Punjab. (Birth-place of Gersh Subhra)

SEHRA   Going on travels or exploring

DADDYJI   `Ji` is added to a name or title as a sign of respect

GOBI PARATHA   A chapatti bread stuffed with grated cauliflower and spices

JALEBI   A popular Indian sweet

LUSSI   A yoghurt and milk drink which can be sweet or salty

TYAA   Paternal uncle

NANIJI   Grandmother

SHALWAR   Loose trousers worn by women

PUTTAR	An affectionate term for children
MANJA	A bed made of a wooden frame and woven rope
NAMASTE	A polite greeting when you meet or depart
KETH	A farmer's field
PUNJAB	A large state in the north of India
NAYEE	Men`s barber
KULFI	Ice cream
MUNDI	Market place
MATAYEE	Indian sweets
CHAPPALS	Sandals
SHABAASH	Well done!
KURTA	A loose cotton shirt worn by men

The Author and the Billu Stories Project

Gersh Subhra left the University of Derby in 2012 after almost 20 years of working with Community and Youth work students as well as managing a Community Regeneration Centre. He is currently studying for a Doctorate and volunteering for Oxfam and the Derby Open Centre, a charity working with children to raise their awareness of different faiths.

Gersh was born in the Punjab region of northern India and left for England in 1964 where his family settled in Coventry. It was in the sixth form at school that Gersh became a volunteer with Oxfam and this continued throughout his time at University in Nottingham. This work with communities led to a career in neighbourhood working, running youth and community centres and then lecturing at Derby University.

Throughout his career Gersh has worked with many volunteers, community activists and projects to tackle local issues and a particular passion has been to widen access to University education for people of all ages and backgrounds.

Throughout his career, Gersh has tried to bring people together to develop projects by using their strengths and resources. This Community Development approach is being adopted in the `Billu Stories Project` and has helped to create a true partnership of friends.

`Billu Leaves India` is the first of a series that Gersh is intending to write and many friends, former students, family and colleagues have offered support in numerous ways. For instance, at the latest count, Gersh has had offers from 150 people who have made a commitment to sell five copies each!

To find out more information about the Billu Stories Project:

gershsubhra@billustories.com
www.billustories.com